KT-466-358

# The Stolen Childhood

## and other dark fairy tales

# The Stolen Childhood

## and other dark fairy tales

Carol Ann Duffy

illustrated by Jane Ray

PUFFIN

For Ella,
with love from Mummy

PUFFIN BOOKS

Published by the Penguin Group
Penguin Books Ltd, 80 Strand, London WC2R 0RL, England
Penguin Putnam Inc., 375 Hudson Street, New York, New York 10014, USA
Penguin Books Australia Ltd, 250 Camberwell Road, Camberwell, Victoria 3124, Australia
Penguin Books Canada Ltd, 10 Alcorn Avenue, Toronto, Ontario, Canada M4V 3B2
Penguin Books India (P) Ltd, 11 Community Centre, Panchsheel Park, New Delhi – 110 017, India
Penguin Books (NZ) Ltd, Cnr Rosedale and Airborne Roads, Albany, Auckland, New Zealand
Penguin Books (South Africa) (Pty) Ltd, 24 Sturdee Avenue, Rosebank 2196, South Africa

Penguin Books Ltd, Registered Offices: 80 Strand, London WC2R 0RL, England

www.penguin.com

First published 2003
10 9 8 7 6 5 4 3 2

Text copyright © Carol Ann Duffy, 2003
Illustrations copyright © Jane Ray, 2003

The moral right of the author and illustrator has been asserted

Set in Cochin 13.5/18pt

Printed in Italy by L.E.G.O.

All rights reserved.
Without limiting the rights under copyright reserved above, no part of this publication may be
reproduced, stored in or introduced into a retrieval system, or transmitted, in any form or by any
means (electronic, mechanical, photocopying, recording or otherwise), without the prior
written permission of both the copyright owner and the above publisher of this book

British Library Cataloguing in Publication Data
A CIP catalogue record for this book is available from the British Library

ISBN 0–141–38012–8

# Contents

# A Little Girl

# Chapter One

A Little Girl lived with her little family in a Doll's House. There was Little Grandma, who had her own room at the top of the house;

Little Grandad, who dozed in a rocking chair in front of the fire all day, even in summer; Little Mummy, who spent most of her time in the kitchen, and Little Twin, the Little Girl's sister, who shared her bedroom and slept above the Little Girl in the top bunk.

Every morning, the little family would eat breakfast together in the kitchen and Little Mummy would serve the weeniest glasses of orange juice, and tiny boiled eggs in teeny egg cups.

After breakfast, Little Grandma would climb up the stairs to her room, sit on a little chair and stare out of the window. Little Grandad rocked himself slowly to sleep in front of the orange and crimson fire while Little Mummy tidied away the breakfast things; and the Little Girl and her Little Twin went to the Drawing Room to play on the little upright piano or read wee books or gaze at the teeny TV in the corner of the room.

The afternoons ticked away, the two children throwing a red ball between them the size of a berry. Every day was the same and whenever the Little Girl asked to go outside her mother shushed her or her grandparents tutted or her sister shook her head.

At night, when the house grew dark, tiny lamps came on in the Doll's House and the little family sat together round the fire until it was time for bed. Then the Little Girl lay in her bottom bunk with her eyes wide open, listening to the thick deep silence of the darkness.

One morning, the Little Girl looked across at her Little Twin and noticed that she seemed smaller. The Little Girl thought that perhaps she was imagining this, but her own tiny black shoes no longer fitted and she had to go about the house barefooted since they were her only pair.

When she sat down for breakfast, she found that her chair was too small for her and her knees scraped on the underside of the kitchen table. She was still hungry after she'd eaten her boiled egg and toast and still thirsty after she'd drained her weeny glass of orange juice, but nobody else seemed to notice these things, so the Little Girl said nothing.

Later, when she asked whether she might go outside, her mother shushed her and her grandparents tutted and her sister shook her head.

That night, as she lay in her bunk, her feet poked out from under her blankets and her head pressed hard against the wall behind her pillow, so she gathered her bedclothes together and stretched out on the floor till morning came.

When the light from outside arrived, she sat up to discover that her head was the same height as her Little Twin's bunk bed. Little Twin started to cry as she looked at her sister's large, pale face, a

The Stolen Childhood

breathing moon, then she ran
downstairs to the kitchen, calling
for Little Mummy.

Chapter Two

From then on, the Little Girl grew apart from the rest of her family. They looked at her strangely as she squeezed herself through the little doors of the Doll's House or stooped and knelt to avoid banging her head on the ceilings. They complained bitterly when they found that she had eaten the entire contents of their little fridge to satisfy her hunger. They whispered to themselves when she knocked over the furniture as she moved about.

Curled in the attic, the largest space in the house, the Little Girl heard the mouse-like squeaks of her family's voices far below. She lifted her arms above her head, carefully raised the red-tiled roof of the Doll's House and climbed outside.

Now that she could stand at her full height, the Little Girl saw that she was as tall as the Doll's House. The chimneys looked like boxes of matches, the front door like a cigarette packet. The windows seemed no bigger than playing cards.

She put her eye to the glass of her grandmother's room. Little Grandma sat in her chair staring out through the window, still and unblinking. She looked, the Little Girl thought, just like a wax doll. She knelt down and peered in through one of the Drawing Room windows on the ground floor. Little Grandad was asleep in his rocking chair in front of the orange and crimson fire that never burnt down. Her sister, Little Twin, was reading the same page of a wee book over and over again.

The Little Girl's eyes filled with tears which fell and splashed against the window like rain. She stretched out and leaned on her elbow to peep into the kitchen where her Little Mummy stood at the table ready to tidy away the breakfast things. More than anything, the Little Girl wished that for once her mother would put on the teeny hat and weeny coat that hung from the hook on the back of the door, walk out of the kitchen, along the hall and out through the front door.

All day, she stared and peeped and squinted through the windows of the Doll's House, noticing the bath the size of a soap dish, the piano the size of a mouth organ, the fridge the size of a choc-ice.

That night, the Little Girl lay down on the floor outside the Doll's House. She could see the tiny lights go out inside the house as she drifted away into sleep.

When she awoke, she was even bigger than before. There was a large comfy-looking bed with plump pillows in the room she was in, a spacious wooden wardrobe full of clothes that fitted her perfectly and several pairs of shoes – just the right size for her feet. She chose a lovely red dress and a pink pair of soft leather boots.

Delicious cooking smells were coming from below. Her Tall Mother smiled at her as she entered the kitchen and said that they'd be having breakfast in the garden. The kitchen window was open and the whole wide wonderful world

stretched endlessly away in the
morning sunlight.

# Chapter Three

So the girl grew and grew and the Doll's House stayed in the corner of her bedroom. She peeped in through its windows at first, but soon she forgot to do this, for she had her own big windows now and she could see the stars. She went outside whenever she wished and travelled far and wide under the sun and under the moon.

In time, she went to live in another house and the Doll's House was packed away and forgotten. She became a woman and had her own family and, though she had her troubles from time to time as everyone does, she was very happy for many years.

One day, the woman looked in the

mirror and saw that she had become old. There were silver threads in her hair and fine lines on her face. Her own daughter was grown up now and had long since moved away and her son was a man who lived in a distant country.

One day, she went up to the attic to store some apples that needed ripening and saw, tucked away in a corner, the old Doll's House.

She knelt before it and peered in through one of the upstairs windows. Little Grandma was sitting in her chair, staring sightlessly out. The woman's heart gave a horrible lurch and her breath came out in a gasp, covering the window with a fine mist. She rubbed at the glass with a corner of her sleeve and Little Grandma stared right through her just as before.

Then the woman looked into the window of her old bedroom and saw that both the little bunk beds were empty, so she crouched lower and peeped into the Drawing Room window. Little Twin sat quietly, reading a wee book, and Little Grandad was asleep in the rocking chair in front of the orange and crimson fire. The woman tapped on the pane with her fingernail but Little Twin didn't look up from her wee book and Little Grandad slept on. The woman felt herself shrinking with longing and regret.

She moved her head till it was level with the kitchen window. Little Mummy stood at the table as she always had. The woman's heart brimmed with love, like a glass filling with the finest wine, and without thinking she banged hard on the window pane with her fists.

Then Little Mummy was waving and smiling at her and had run down the hall to fling open the front door and she felt her Little Twin's tiny hand in hers, pulling her inside, and heard the small excited clucks of Little Grandma and Little Grandad as they walked towards her.

The door closed behind her with a neat click.

That night, the Little Girl stood at her bedroom window as her little family slept. Outside the Doll's House, planets glowed and shone like giant apples far out in the endless universe.

# Invisible

# Chapter One

A boy lived happily with his parents on the edge of a village in the very last cottage before the forest began. His mother worked in the woods, collecting chestnuts, hazelnuts and walnuts. His father laboured as a woodcutter, chopping up tree trunks and branches for furniture and fuel. But one terrible day the father had an accident in the forest and died.

The boy and his mother wept as the father was buried in a coffin nailed together from wood he had cut down himself. They grieved for two winters, but when spring came again, the boy's mother met a new man and married him.

When his mother and stepfather came

home from their honeymoon, the boy was waiting for them. His mother ran to him and kissed him, but his stepfather looked straight through him as though he wasn't there. When bedtime came, the boy kissed his mother goodnight, but when he looked to do the same to his stepfather, the man ignored him and carried on reading his book.

The boy climbed the stairs and lay on his narrow bed. The moon stooped and stared at him through the window with its scarred old face. The boy got up and looked out at the forest where his father had died, where alder, ash, aspen, willow, beech, cherry, poplar, oak, birch, hawthorn, hazel, juniper, lime, rowan, pine, elm, apple and yew whispered in darkness; but his sorrow had hardened now and his tears were like small glass stones in his eyes.

The boy slept late and when he came down for breakfast, his mother had already left to collect nuts in the forest. His stepfather was writing letters at the kitchen table and barely glanced at him when he sat down with his milk and his bread roll.

The boy ate in silence, conscious of the small slurps he made as he drank.

The air around his stepfather seemed dark and heavy, as though he made his own weather. He was a handsome man, unsmiling and strong. There were black hairs on the back of his hands.

The man looked up and the boy jumped, worried that he'd been caught staring. But the stepfather said nothing, took his coat from the back of the kitchen door and went out, banging it hard behind him. The boy went to the mirror on the wall and stared at his pale thin face.

Chapter _Two_

A sunny day came and the boy knew there was to be a trip to the travelling fair that was on in the big town. He woke early and washed himself and brushed his hair and got dressed in his favourite clothes. But when he came downstairs, he saw that his mother had been crying. His stepfather walked past him without a word and went outside to wait for his wife by the gate. The mother couldn't look her son in the eyes.

She pressed some coins into his palm and told him that he wasn't to accompany them to the fair, but was to stay behind and buy himself some lunch from the village shop. They would be back late, she said, and he was to be in bed when they returned.

The boy shouted at her and threw the coins at her feet, but she shook her head and hurried to the gate to join her husband. The boy left the coins glinting on the floor and promised himself that he would go hungry rather than spend them. He stuffed his pockets with nuts from his mother's collecting basket and ran to the woods.

Dusk came and the forest sulked and darkened. The boy grew cold and climbed down from the branch he'd been sitting on. He made his way back along the path, passing the stumps of trees cut down by his dead father.

There was no one at home.

He ate some fruit from the bowl, then went up to bed.

Hours later, the noise of his mother and stepfather returning to the cottage woke him. His door was ajar and he saw them go past on the way to their bedroom. The lamp on the landing lit up their faces, but they did not look in on him.

The days and weeks and months went by, until spring, summer and autumn were gone and it was winter again. The boy moved around the house like a ghost and if ever he caught his mother's eye she looked away.

He had stopped going to school, but nobody seemed to notice; and when his stepfather met the schoolteacher in the village inn, nothing was said.

One day, the boy came into the kitchen for an apple and saw his stepfather standing there. The boy reached for an apple in the bowl but as he did so the stepfather's big hand swooped down and seized it. He looked into the man's eyes and heard the crunch as he bit into the apple, but the man strolled past him, brushing against him as though he wasn't there, as though he was nothing.

The boy went to the mirror again, but when he gazed there he could only see the reflection of the kitchen – his mother's empty collecting basket on the table, the man's heavy coat hanging on the hook of the door.

He leaned closer to the mirror and breathed, but the glass stayed as bright and clear as before. He pressed the flat palm of his hand against it, but although he could feel the coldness of the mirror he could see nothing of himself.

Terrified, with his heart jerking in his chest, the boy ran upstairs to his mother's bedroom. He sat down at the stool in front of the dressing table and stared wildly into each of the three mirrors there. His face was in none of them.

He fled downstairs and into the sitting room where his mother and stepfather sat. In her arms, his mother held a new baby, carefully wrapped in a soft white blanket. He called his mother's name, but she bent low over the baby's head and made a shushing sound. The stepfather stood up and walked towards him, tall and brooding. The boy backed away and the man shut the door in his face.

And now the boy was truly invisible. He had grown in the year since his mother had married again and his clothes were tight-fitting or too short. Since no one could see him, he put on a big old shirt of his father's and went about in that.

He left home in the morning and spent his days in the forest. In the evenings, he returned to the cottage, taking some food – bread or fruit or nuts – up to his room and eating it there.

Sometimes he stood at the side of the baby's crib and looked down at his half-brother, but he was always quiet as he knew the child could not see him. If he passed his mother in the house, she busied herself at something, or buried her face in the baby's neck. To his stepfather, he was less than a shadow on the stairs. At night, he lay alone on his bed, hearing his mother cry and the man shout.

# Chapter Three

Time passed. One day, as he walked in the woods, the boy, who was tall now and broad-shouldered, saw a girl of his own age sitting on the branch of his favourite tree and swinging her legs.

So used was he to being invisible, that he stood and stared at her from the path. But the girl turned her bright hazel eyes on his and laughed at him. Then she reached into the dense foliage of the tree, rustled about there, and tossed him the shiniest, reddest apple in the world. He caught it low with his left hand, like a catch at cricket.

Then he remembered that he had on only his father's old shirt, which came to his knees, so he turned and ran away into the forest, clutching the apple. But the girl jumped down from the tree and chased him, and as she was a faster runner than the boy, she soon caught up with him, and she grabbed him by his shirt-tails and kissed him on the lips.

When he woke the next morning, the boy climbed up to the small attic and found the chest that contained his dead father's things. He put on some soft corduroy trousers, a clean linen shirt and a beautiful leather jacket which still held the scent of wood-shavings and pine. He took out his father's watch, set it to the right time and put it on his wrist. He pulled on warm socks and good boots.

He went downstairs to the kitchen where his mother was preparing breakfast. She stared at him and tears scalded her eyes and he knew that she saw him. But the girl from the woods was waiting by the gate and he went out to meet her.

He came home late, under the light of stars that had taken years to arrive, and went to his bed. In the morning, he went off with the girl again, and he felt his mother drink him in with her eyes as she watched him go.

After a month and a day of this, he arrived home one night and found his stepfather in the kitchen. The man looked older and smaller now that the boy had grown so tall and fit, and his black hair was greying.

He shouted to the boy that he needn't think he could come and go as he pleased and with a shock the boy realized that the man was looking at him at last. But he pushed his stepfather easily away and went up to his bed.

As he lay there, he heard the man's yells and his mother's wails. Outside his window, the moon scudded high up in the clouds, like a coin tossed for heads or tails.

# Chapter Four

The next day, the boy woke early and for the first time made breakfast for his mother and her child and himself. As they were eating, the stepfather came in, but the boy didn't glance at him and eventually the man went awkwardly away.

That night, when the boy came home, he brought the girl with him and cooked a meal for them all, so that she could meet his mother and her child. The stepfather came in again, just as the boy was slicing up a pie, but the boy ignored him until the man muttered to himself and disappeared.

Every morning, the boy rose early to prepare breakfast and each night he came home with the girl and cooked supper. He worked in the forest now, chopping wood as his father had done.

When the girl looked at him, she had love in her hazel eyes, like a light, and as it shone on him he grew stronger and more handsome. The mother stared at her two sons and began to notice all the ways in which they were alike.

There was no more shouting or crying in the house and the boy resolutely treated his stepfather as though he were invisible. The sullen man kept to himself and bothered nobody.

One day he vanished altogether, taking his coat from the hook on the back of the door, and it was as though he had never been there at all.

The young man worked hard in the forest to keep food on the table for the family and the girl took the collecting basket from the mother to gather chestnuts, hazelnuts and walnuts.

They were all very happy and as his small half-brother grew, the young man made sure to watch over him ever after, with the light of love in his eyes.

# The
# Stolen
## Childhood

# Chapter One

A stepmother lived with her dead husband's young daughter. The girl was sweet-natured and lovely but the stepmother had a heart that had soured and shrivelled under her black frock. Her hair had dried and rusted on her head and she took pleasure in nothing.

Day after day, from a high window, she watched her step-daughter as she played in the garden and the stepmother's blood clogged with envy as she saw the young girl chasing a butterfly or turning cartwheels or singing to herself in the arms of the apple tree. More than anything, the stepmother yearned and burned to be young again.

One day, a stranger came to their village and took a room at the Traveller's Inn. The stepmother, staring as usual from her high window, saw the stranger walking in the lane. He was tall with black hair and as the woman gazed down at him he glanced up and spied her.

His eyes were hard and green like emeralds and with one look he saw into her dark soul and knew what she wanted.

'Come to me,' he said and she heard him and jumped, as though a poker were stirring the burnt coals and ashes of her heart.

She hurried down the stairs,

out of the house and into the lane to stand beside him.

Close up she could see that there was no kindness in his face and she shivered. He was holding a pair of sharp silver scissors.

'I can give you what you most want,' he said. 'Take these scissors and cut the shadow from the first young person you find asleep. Then you must snip off your own shadow and throw it over the young person without waking them. Their youth will be yours at once and they will be as old as you are now.'

'What must I pay you for this?'

asked the stepmother, because she knew very well there would be a price.

'You will be my bride,' he answered, 'on the happiest day of your life.'

The stepmother gave a dry laugh and thought that the man was joking, but she agreed to his strange bargain and took the scissors. He walked rapidly away down the lane and quite soon after that he left the village.

# Chapter Two

The stepmother went into the garden holding the scissors which glittered in her hand in the sunlight.

Her young stepdaughter was stretched out on the lawn with her straw hat over her face, fast asleep in the warm buttery sun. Her shadow lay on the grass beside her, so cool and dark that already the daisies there had started to close.

The stepmother knelt down, silent as poison, and cut along the whole length of the girl's shadow. A breeze blew under it and lifted it gently but the stepmother snatched at it, crumpling it up and stuffing it in her skirt pocket. It felt like the softest silk.

Then the stepmother stood and

saw her own long shadow at her feet. She bent down and with a snap and a snip she cut it off. She lifted her heavy, leathery shadow and tossed it over the sleeping girl, then turned and ran towards the house to look in the mirror. Her step felt lighter and for the first time in years she noticed all the different smells of the garden as she ran.

The stepdaughter felt something heavy and sour-smelling upon her and opened her eyes in fright. It was dark. She screamed and tried to jump up but her body felt stiff and strange and her back ached.

She sat up and pushed the shadow away from her and it lay in a heap like an old black coat.

'How horrible!' cried the girl.

She touched her throat. Her voice was different, deeper and harsher, not like a child's voice at all. She looked at her hands. They were like a pair of crumpled gloves, several sizes too big, the skin loose and creased over the bones.

She stood up slowly, holding the small of her back, and heard the waxy creak of her knees. Truly scared now, she hurried as fast as

she could, a bit out of breath, to
look in the mirror.

# Chapter Three

The mirror was a full-length one and hung in the shadowy hall. The stepmother was standing before it and she turned as she heard the sound of her stepdaughter behind her. Both of them stared at each other in disbelief and then the stepmother began to laugh, the light easy laugh of a young girl.

'Look at yourself!' she cried and pulled her stepdaughter to the mirror.

A middle-aged face stared back from the glass, grey-haired and lined. The stepdaughter's teeth felt strange and uncomfortable in her mouth and when she touched them with her tongue she realized that they were false. She began to cough and the bitter taste of tobacco scalded the back of her throat. She turned to her stepmother.

Her stepmother was smaller, with soft hair the colour of a conker and skin as delicate as the petal of a rose. She was jumping up and down and clapping her hands.

'It worked! It worked!' she cried. 'I am young again and YOU have all my years!'

Then the stepmother spun round and ran back into the sunshine and the poor step-daughter fell to the floor in the dark hall and sobbed bitterly.

# Chapter Four

Summer turned, as it has to do, into autumn and autumn soon became winter.

It was the stepdaughter now

who stood at the window, a shawl round her cold stiff bones, watching the village children throw snowballs in the field on the other side of the lane.

She wondered why her young stepmother never played with the others, why she never helped to make a snowman – pushing a snowball along till it doubled and trebled and quadrupled in size, creaking under her mittens. And why she never hopped and whistled her way to school with the other children or pressed her nose to the toy-shop window or scraped a stick along the green railings of the park. What was the point of her stepmother being young at all?

A fierce headache tightened round her brow, deepening the frowns and creases on her papery skin, and she turned away from the window and went to lie down on the bed in her hushed dull room. She was always tired now.

She took out her teeth and put them in a glass of water on the bedside table. They grinned away at her as though Death himself had come to call.

The stepmother was downstairs in the kitchen eating a huge plate of jam sandwiches and washing them down with lemonade. Nowadays, she was always eating.

She ate breakfast, elevenses, lunch, afternoon tea, dinner and supper. In between meals she guzzled cakes, crackers, crumpets, crumbles, scones, biscuits, gingerbreads, shortbreads, wafers, pastries, fancies, gateaux, turnovers, tarts, flans, puffs, snaps, buns and doughnuts.

*How wonderful it is*, she thought to herself, *to have an appetite again*.

She pulled on her boots and went for a walk in the snow, ignoring the shouts of the children playing in the field.

'Youth,' she sneered to herself, 'is wasted on the young.'

She walked for miles, breathing in the clean cold air and not feeling the faintest bit tired, working up a good hunger for dinner.

She grabbed a fistful of snow and sucked at it, gasping at the cold. She was young again! Young! Her skin and her eyes and her hair sparkled in the hard white winter light.

# Chapter Five

Winter turned to spring then summer then autumn then winter then spring then summer . . .

The stepmother was taller now

and beautiful and many young men came to the house to visit her. They brought flowers and perfume and chocolates and told her that they adored her, that she was the loveliest young girl in the village, that her lips were rubies and her eyes were sapphires and that each little nail on the tips of her fingers was a pearl.

'I am in the springtime of my life,' gloated the stepmother. 'Again!'

Her stepdaughter watched the young men come and go from her window, but none of them so much as glanced up at the sad old woman with the dull eyes and the yellowing teeth.

One young man, the step-daughter thought, was handsomer and jollier than all the rest and her heart, tired as it was, would skip a beat as though it had almost remembered something, whenever she saw him.

At night she would dream that she was dancing and laughing in his arms, a girl once more. But when she woke up she was alone, brittle and aching in the mothbally shroud of her nightgown.

As the summer passed, she noticed that the young man came

more and more often to the house to visit her stepmother and that the other boys had drifted away.

On the first day of autumn her stepmother and the young man came before her and told her that they were to be married. Her tired heart sank like a stone in her chest as she looked at the young man and she knew then that she loved him, but she kissed her stepmother and wished her happiness.

'Oh, I will be happy,' answered the stepmother. 'My wedding day will be the happiest day of my life.'

The stepmother had decided to be married at Christmas. The days fell from the calendar like leaves from the trees and, quicker than the snip of scissors, it was the morning of Christmas Eve.

The wedding was to be at noon and already the bellringers were swinging from their ropes, sending the warm bronze voices of the bells across the frozen fields. The bride was to be driven from the house to the church in a white carriage pulled by a chestnut horse. The stepdaughter was to ride behind her in a plain wooden carriage.

As the bells chimed eleven o'clock, the stepdaughter was standing in the lane waiting for the carriages to arrive. The cold bit through her dark winter coat into her bones.

'Here I am!' Her stepmother stood at the door of the house in a dress of silver and gold. 'How do I look?'

'You look good enough to eat,' said a harsh voice from the lane.

The stepdaughter saw the shock and surprise on her stepmother's face and turned to see who had spoken.

A tall man with a mean face and

fierce green eyes had appeared from nowhere and stood staring intensely at the bride. 'Our carriage will be here soon.'

'Our carriage?' said the stepmother. 'You must be mistaken!'

All the colour had drained from her face until she was paler than the late white roses that she carried in her hands.

'Come,' said the stranger impatiently. 'You know very well what is to happen today.'

'Today is to be the happiest day of my life,' replied the stepmother in a trembling voice. 'I am to marry the young man who loves me.'

'You are to marry me, my beauty,' said the tall man, 'and you can forget about love. Come!'

'Marry you?' said the bride. 'You?' She laughed nervously.

The sound of horses' hooves clattered suddenly in the lane and the stepmother ran to her stepdaughter and clutched at her arm. She had started to cry and the stepdaughter could see that she was shaking with fear.

'Who is he?' she asked the terrified bride.

The carriages had arrived, but

one was a closed ebony carriage drawn by four black horses who steamed and snorted in the lane.

'Get into the carriage!' said the stranger as he flung open the door.

'No! No! You can't make me!' The stepmother was sobbing now and quite wild with terror and the stepdaughter felt real dread, colder than ice, chilling her heart.

'Who is he? Tell me!' she said again.

'For the last time,' said the man, 'get into the carriage.'

But the stepmother looked into

his eyes and saw all the badness of this world and the next and would not go. She shook her head.

# Chapter Six

The stranger gave a twisted smile and stared hard at the bride.

'You have broken your promise,' he said. 'Put your hand in

the pocket of your dress.'

The stepmother did as she was told and pulled out a small piece of crumpled black silk. She gave a little scream and dropped it and it floated down to the ground and landed at her stepdaughter's feet.

Then the tall man pulled off his coat and the stepdaughter saw that it was the old black coat that had nearly suffocated her when she was a child. With a quick movement the stranger threw it over her stepmother, completely covering her lovely gold and silver dress.

'Don't!' she screamed. 'I'll

come! I'll come!'

'Too late,' said the man, and he climbed into the ebony carriage. The four black horses tossed their heads and neighed and began to move away.

'Come back!' screeched the stepmother, but the carriage gathered speed, reached the bend at the top of the lane and vanished. The clatter of hooves faded into the distance.

The stepmother flung away the coat and turned to face her stepdaughter. 'Help me!' she said. 'What am I to do?'

Her stepdaughter was staring

at her in horror. The stepmother's beautiful dress hung in tattered grey rags from her bony shoulders. Her hair had turned white and clumps of it had fallen from her head, leaving some of it bald. Her mouth had shrunk inwards in a small wrinkled O of disappointment, as though her lips were mourning her vanished teeth. Her body shrivelled and stooped till she looked like a question mark asking, *Why? Why? Why?*

She was twice as old as before and her voice when she spoke was the dusty croak of a crone. 'Why do you stare at me?'

Then she clutched at her throat and gaped at her stepdaughter. Colour had flooded back into the stepdaughter's hair, a glowing red-blonde, and the girl was smiling at her with perfect white teeth.

'What is happening to me?' she said and when she heard the light music of her own voice she laughed with delight. 'Stepmother! I am myself again!'

She felt her young lungs breathing easily and her heart opened like a flower in her breast.

There were running footsteps in the lane and it was the bridegroom, out of breath and looking for the bride. He glanced curiously at the old witch, bent double by the ditch, coughing and cursing, but as soon as he saw the girl he had eyes only for her.

'Your bride has gone,' she said to him.

'I am sorry to hear that,' he said politely, but his eyes burned with sudden love as he looked at her.

There was a strange noise from the ditch and they both turned to see the old black coat lying in a heap on the road. There was no sign of the stepmother, but a sudden gust of wind blew a handful of ashes, grey and gritty, over the fields.

'Your bride has gone forever,' repeated the girl.

'My bride was lovely,' said the young man, 'but you are truly the most beautiful girl I have ever seen in my life.'

The girl looked down at her hands and saw the light of youth that glowed under her skin and she felt the force and energy of life itself rise up from the tingling tips of her toes so that all she wanted to do was run!

'Catch me if you can!' She laughed at the young man and took to her heels, flinging off her heavy winter coat as she went.

With a shout, laughing himself, he chased her, never quite catching her, his pounding feet landing on her slim fast shadow as she ran before him.